except if

For Ed

*

With special thanks to Nami and Ann

ATHENEUM BOOKS FOR YOUNG READERS

An imprint of Simon & Schuster Children's Publishing Division

1230 Avenue of the Americas, New York, New York 10020

Copyright © 2011 by Jim Averbeck

ATHENEUM BOOKS FOR YOUNG READERS is a registered trademark of Simon & Schuster, Inc.

For information about special discounts for bulk purchases, please contact Simon & Schuster Special Sales at 1-866-506-1949 or business@simonandschuster.com.

The Simon & Schuster Speakers Bureau can bring authors to your live event. For more information or to book an event, contact the Simon & Schuster Speakers Bureau at 1-866-248-3049 or visit our website at www.simonspeakers.com.

Book design by Ann Bobco

The text for this book is set in Modern No. 20.

The illustrations for this book are rendered in oil pastel on Rives BFK, digitally transferred to Arches hot press paper, and painted with watercolor.

Manufactured in China

0411 SCP

10 9 8 7 6 5 4 3 2

Library of Congress Cataloging-in-Publication Data

Averbeck, Jim.

Except if / Jim Averbeck. — 1st ed.

p. cm.

Summary: An egg is just an egg except if, after hatching, it becomes something else.

ISBN 978-1-4169-9544-9 (hardcover)

[1. Eggs—Fiction. 2. Animals—Infancy—Fiction.] I. Title.

PZ7.A933816Ex 2011

[E]— dc22   2009052489

except
if

by jim averbeck

atheneum books for young readers
new york * london * toronto * sydney

An egg is not a baby bird,

but it will become one

except if

it becomes a baby snake

who will slither along the ground on its belly

except if

it is a baby lizard

who will scurry up the wall
on sticky feet and
eat flies

except if

it grows into a dinosaur

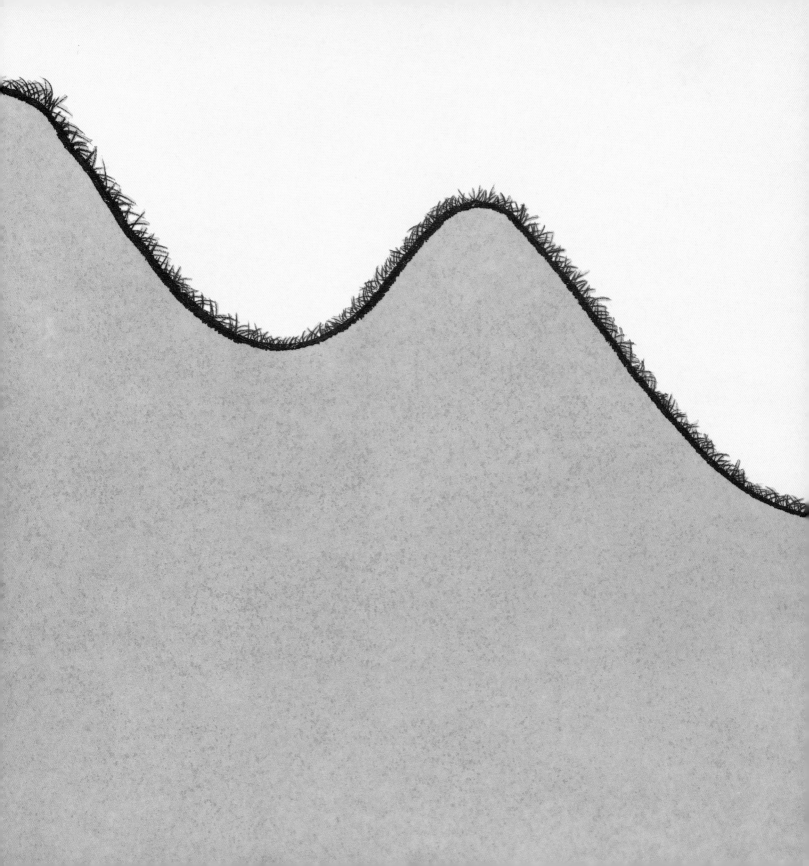

who will stand as high as the hills
(and eat whatever it wants)

except if

it is a fossil

whose jaws will form
a craggy cliff ledge,
sharp and bare,

except if

it shelters a soft, downy nest

that will rest
empty between
rocky teeth

except if

it is spring,

when it will cradle
a pale blue egg,

which will not necessarily
become a baby bird

except if it does.